Christmas in the **Kalahari**

CODY'S CRAFT CORNER

Wherever you go in the world Christmas looks different, tastes different, and is celebrated in different ways.

Here in the Kalahari we meerkats may not have snow and pine trees, but who needs snow when we have sand, a plentiful supply of insects, and each other!

Try this fabulous family craft activity for even more festive fun. These delightful and delicious decorations can be made using all locally sourced materials.

HOW TO

1. Gather as many bugs as you want (Be aware. If you try this activity with the kits, expect them to eat more than they save!)

2. Find an attractive nearby tree or cactus to decorate.

3. Place each bug on the tree (you may need to give each a little food to tempt them to stay put).

4. Feed to the kits as fun-sized snacks when boredom strikes (usually once grown ups get talking).

36

Millipedes
(Giant ones!)

This huge millepede makes a versatile decoration that can be draped artfully over branches, or coiled into attractive shapes. Contrary to popular belief a millepede does not have a million legs, but nearer to 256.

Toktokkies
(Fog-basking Beetle)

What these black or dark brown beetles lack in colour they make up for with their pleasant 'tocking' noise. They can be found on top of sand dunes in foggy weather, and are easily recognised by their habit of standing on their heads.

(May be improved with glitter)

Scorpion
(Any kind you can catch)

Scorpions make the most wonderful Christmas decorations. They can be hung individually, but are most effective when strung together in long chains. They are especially magical when lit with a UV torch, which makes them glow bright blue.

(Remove the stingers for young kits)

White Lady Spider
(Tap dancer)

This beautiful spider can be a tricky one to catch, but is sure to look stunning on top of any tree. A perfect star substitute.

KALAHARI CANDY CANES

Home-made Xmas treats - healthier, yet cheaper!

Serves 25

25 assorted snakes (whatever variety you can catch)

1 tin (edible) red paint

1 tin (edible) white paint

2 paint brushes

Begin by catching all 25 snakes - and securing them in a basket with a tight-fitting lid.

Holding each snake tightly, paint first with white paint. You may need two coats to fully cover.

Once dry, paint the white snakes with red diagonal stripes.

Bend each snake into a candy cane shape and hang on tree or cactus. GOOD LUCK!

First
published
in 2019 by Two Hoots,
this edition published
in 2020 by Two Hoots
an imprint of Pan Macmillan
The Smithson, 6 Briset Street,
London, EC1M 5NR
Associated companies throughout the world
www.panmacmillan.com
ISBN: 978-1-5098-5730-2

1 3 5 7 9 8 6 4 2
A CIP catalogue record for this book is available from the British Library. Printed in China.
The illustrations in this book were created using anything that came to hand.
www.twohootsbooks.com

For Sandy

For Cody

It's nearly Christmas in the Kalahari, and all the meerkats are busy.

Sunny's mum and dad are
busy cleaning the burrow,

Sunny's brothers and sisters
are busy putting up the Christmas
decorations, and Sunny's aunts
and uncles are busy cooking.

EVERYONE is very excited.

Everyone except for Sunny.

He has been reading all about how to have the Perfect Christmas, and this does NOT look perfect.

PERFECT
MAGAZINE

XMAS EXTRA

IN THIS ISSUE:
- PERFECT festive food
- PERFECT decorations
- PERFECT gifts

Have a PERFECT Christmas

See how it SHOULD be done!

Everything you need for the PERFECT Christmas

So Sunny packs his bag and sets off to find somewhere more Christmassy, just like in his magazine.

His first stop is at his pen pal Kev's.

Kev is having a lovely Christmas, but it all looks a bit like the Kalahari to Sunny. So he says goodbye, and carries on with his search.

The decorations are amazing at Trevor's,
and there are plenty of trees, but it doesn't look
anything like the Christmas in his magazine.
Where is all the snow?

Sunny hates getting wet.

This looks more like it!

Wishing you a COOL Christmas

This looks more like it!

But it's a lot colder than he had expected,
and not a Christmas tree in sight.

At last! Christmas trees.

MINISTRY OF CHRISTMAS TREES

Once each tree has been decorated and inspected by the supervisor it should be checked off the chart below by ...ering with the stickers provided.

...target for ....
................................150 Trees

...achieved .... Supervisor Signature ....

Too many Christmas trees . . .

1. THE PERFECT WEATHER: Must be snow. Deep and crisp. ✓
2. THE PERFECT TREE: Must be tastefully decorated. ✓
3. THE PERFECT PRESENTS: There must be a HUGE pile. ✓
4. THE PERFECT DINNER: Must include well-boiled sprouts. ✓
5. THE PERFECT MUSIC: Christmas Carols.

On the night before Christmas Sunny arrives somewhere PERFECT. The snow is falling (outside), everyone is singing, there is a beautifully decorated tree, plenty of presents and a HUGE Christmas dinner with all the trimmings (even sprouts).

It should be perfect . . .

Q: What do mice eat for Christmas dinner?

A: Cheese and crackers!

. . . but something *still* isn't right.

I miss you all VERY much — love from Sunny
xxxxx
xxxx

To
The BIG Meerkat Mob
Sandy Burrow
The Dunes
Kalahari Desert
Under the BIG BLUE SKY

It's Christmas morning in the Kalahari.

The meerkats should be excited about opening their presents, but they are too busy missing Sunny.

Until . . .

HAPPY CHRISTMAS!

Astrid & Mina

PERFECT MAGAZINE'S

Perfect Christmas Dinner

FOLLOW THIS MENU PLAN FOR A PERFECT CHRISTMAS DINNER

YUK!!

STARTERS:
Smoked Salmon
or
Pâté
or
Prawn Cocktail
or
Chestnut Soup

Smoked
Centipede
Paté

MAINS:
Roast Turkey
or
Roast Beef
or
Roast Goose
or
Roast Nuts

Roast Reptile
(snake or lizard)

SIDES:
Boiled Brussels Sprouts
and
Roast Potatoes
and
Roast Parsnips
and
Roast Carrots

Steamed spiders
Mashed millipedes

DESSERT:
Christmas Pudding
and/or
Mince Pies
and/or
Figgy Pudding
with
Brandy Butter
or
Cream

or Scorpion Pudding
Buggy Pudding

YOUR SHOPPING NOTES...
Best dune for lizards is
behind big cactus

DON'T FORGET TO GET
SPICY ants FOR SNACKS

EMILY GRAVETT has a rare talent for creating exceptional books for children. A winner of two CILIP Kate Greenaway Medals, Emily first sprang into the limelight with the ground-breaking *Wolves* in 2005, which has been followed by such modern classics as *Meerkat Mail*, *Tidy* and *Again!* and the fabulous Bear and Hare series for younger readers.

Emily also won the inaugural BookTrust Storytime Prize in 2019 with her book *Cyril and Pat*. All of her books are unique and feature endearing, beautifully drawn characters that touch the heart and tickle the funny bone.